THE GIFT OF GOD

Revised 2025

Dr. Alice James

Publishing

Table of Contents

Foreword

Boaz, The Gift of God, is a heartfelt book written from the depths of Alice James heart. This compelling book will pierce the soul of everyone who reads it. You see, every woman who dreams to one day be married, would love to have as her soulmate a husband who treats her like a queen and cherishes every moment, they are together. That dream is not impossible.

In this book, Alice takes you on a journey where she had to travel through the storm, rain, hail, sleet and finally the sunshine to get her Boaz. This storybook testimony was written to encourage you to always put your faith in the Lord no matter how bleak things look in your life. You may not see your Boaz with the physical eye, but Hebrews 11:1 says, *"Now faith is the substance of things hoped for, the evidence of things not seen."*

In Love with Christ,
Elder Debbie E. Hawkins
First Lady, Voices of Faith Ministry

Introduction

As I lay asleep one night, the Holy Spirit quickened my heart and soul and awakened me at 3:00 in the morning. "Get a pen and a piece of paper!" he said. As I picked up a pen and paper, a wonderful love story, which paralleled to Ruth's story in the Old Testament, unfolded before my eyes. This book developed into Boaz, The Gift of God, and was written to encourage the lonely and brokenhearted. As you read pages of this book, you will find a love story, my love story, about my journey through life searching for my soul mate while enduring the hardships of broken and bad relationships. Through all my heartbreaking trials, I learned to lean fully, to trust, and to depend on God. Boaz, in the Old Testament, was a wealthy man who became the redeemer of Ruth, a virtuous woman who loved her mother-in-law.

Boaz, The Gift of God, is a riveting account of one woman's journey through pain, trials, and troubles while looking for genuine happiness and true love. This heart-warming book will move you to tears, inspire you, and help you through life while encouraging you in your walk with God. This book expounds on the truth of

God's Word that will leave you thirsty for more of His Spirit in your life.

Boaz, The Gift of God, is a book for everyone, from the single individual seeking love, to the married couple that is hoping to rekindle the love, passion, and romance in their marriage. Dr. James opens up her heart and reveals the hurt of her past by sharing painful personal experiences and guides us to a place in God where we can totally trust Him to meet all our needs and bring our soulmates into our lives. These revelations will help the reader to reflect on the very real presence of God in our own lives.

Boaz, The Gift of God, is a truly eye-opening, inspirational book that will challenge you to seek for, and to follow, the path that God has designed for your life and to enjoy the blessings that are sure to follow.

Enjoy this easy guide to find the Will of God for you and be confident that God may want you to be single and to serve Him as a single person. Or God may allow the Boaz in your life to be revealed.

My Desire For You

As I open my heart and share my innermost secrets with you, my deepest desire is that God will reveal His perfect plan for your life. I have great hope and vision for this book—just as loving parents long to see their children grow and prosper, I know this work is something profoundly special, and I pray it touches your life in a meaningful way. I hope that every reader finds encouragement, grows in their faith, and discovers the Boaz that God has divinely intended for them. May this book be a source of blessing, guiding you to make strong, faith-filled, and life-changing decisions.

--Dr. Alice James

Dedication

This book is dedicated to my parents, who both passed away before I finished it but were blessed to meet my Boaz, Roy. My mom said many times and told everyone that Roy was just like a son to her.

Mama and Daddy, thank you for all your encouragement and for believing in me. Thank you for your strong convictions, strength, character, and unwavering love and faith in God. Thank you for instructing me on how to be the virtuous wife that God wants me to be. Thank you for all the lessons of life that you taught me and for instilling in me the faith to trust in God because "He will always see you through."

Mama and Daddy, I love you always-…
-Your Baby Girl, Alice Marie

To my wonderful son, Cliford (Clif"), who is the other "Boaz" in my life, for his intelligence and encouraging words and for recognizing Boaz before I recognized him.

This book is especially dedicated to my husband, my Boaz, Roy, for without you, it would never have been.

Acknowledgments

First and foremost, I acknowledge Christ and His Precious Holy Spirit for preparing and sending me Boaz; for without you, Christ, in my life, I don't know where I would be.

To my wonderful big sister, Joyce, who doesn't know it, but much of what I learned in my life came as a result of her being there for me to encourage and guide me. In many ways, she inspired me and subconsciously contributed a significant amount to the content of this book. Joyce, you will never know the love, respect and honor I truly have for you. You are now the backbone of our family.

To my niece, Nisie, who I dearly loved and who passed away before the completion of this book but who had the opportunity to grow and love Roy and who was a strong supporter of what we believe in. Nisie, you were a strong supporter of our family; we miss you dearly.

To my editors, Ginger and my dear friend Katie, whose unwavering moral support, exceptional talent, and continuous guidance made the completion of this project possible. It's incredible to think that this journey began back in 2005, and here we are today, with a finished work—thanks to your dedication, insight, and genuine belief in my story. Ginger, I'll never forget the first time you read my draft and said, "You have a story to tell!" Your encouragement, along with the countless drafts, do-overs, thoughtful questions, and challenges along the way, kept me motivated to see it through. I am profoundly grateful for your knowledge, skills, and belief in me. Thank you from the bottom of my heart.

To my best friends who have been there for me always and are never afraid to tell me the truth, even when it hurts: Sandra Tyson, Zakiyyah "Joy" Russell, Nicole Skidmore, and Dynetta Woods. Guys, you are the best. Thank you for being there for me.

A *special thanks* to Elder Keith Richard, my consultant advisor; without him, this book would not have been successful. Elder Richard, thank you for your direction, advice, suggestions and guidance.

To all my many other family members who put up with me: Calvin Collier, Sallie Collier, Willie Collier, Antoinette Stewart,

Calvin Collier, Jr. Kenyetta Collier, Gary Stewart, April Montgomery.

The Book Cover Review Team

Evangelist Christine Banks, Elder Tonya Carter, Mrs. Amy Chandler, Evangelist Sylvia Dickson, Dr. Joyce Edwards, Ms. Raenata Hamilton, Ms. Creola Johnson, Evangelist Cassandra Lang, Minister Ginger London, Ms. Charise Patterson, Ms. Joy Russell, Ms. Nicole Skidmore, Sister Sandra Tyson and Mrs. Dynetta Woods.

Thanks for your honesty, direction, and support.

The Day of the Lord and afterward, I will pour out my Spirit on all people. Your sons and daughters will prophesy, your old men and women will dream dreams, your men will see visions.

—Joel 2:28 NIV

I had the same dream that every woman has, whether she is Christian or not; I wanted to find my Boaz. I'm sure you know and remember the rich man in the Bible who took Ruth as his wife and treated her like a queen even though she was poor and destitute. This was the same Ruth of lowly origins who eventually became the mother of King David's lineage.

Like most women who followed the old saying, I *was "looking for love in all the wrong places."* I was guilty, just like millions of other single women, of looking for my knight in shining armor in inappropriate, even dangerous, places. You know what I am talking about, questionable venues such as nightclubs and bars.

In this day of women's lib and equal rights for everyone, we as a people have lost something very important. We have lost an understanding of women's impact on every man's life. We have forgotten how to nurture and support our men and how to encourage them to achieve self-esteem. We have forgotten how to help them become all that they can be.

Instead, we continue to argue, demand, and nag our men to try and get what we want from them, or to try and change them. We have become the kind of women God warned men about in the Bible when He said in Proverbs 21:9, *"It is better to dwell in a corner of the housetop than with a brawling woman in a wide house."* Or as seen in Proverbs 21:19, *"It is better to dwell in the wilderness than with a contentious and an angry woman."* This woman is argumentative, combative, or frequently engages in disputes or disagreements.

Are you this type of woman? As women, we have always believed "we know how to make a man become the man that we want him to be." We continually tear our men down instead of lifting them up and emphasizing that they can be the kind of men that God intended, i.e., the lovers, the supporters, the friends, the strong men of God and the strong men of valor. We see even in the Bible that God sought a man of quality for Ruth, as seen in Ruth Chapter 4, where the faithfulness of Ruth, the kindness of Boaz, and the provision of God for those who trust in Him are described. It also serves as a reminder of God's redemptive plan and how He can achieve good out of difficult circumstances.

Ruth's unwavering patience and faith in God's plan greatly inspired me. Despite her own challenges, she remained steadfast in her trust in God, which made me question whether I possessed the same level of faith and resilience. Considering my intelligence and hard work, I wondered why I couldn't take control of my desires and pursue them on my own terms.

The Old Testament, specifically Proverbs 31:10, questions and searches for a righteous, honorable, and moral woman. It asks, *"Who can find a virtuous woman, for her price [is] far above rubies."* Finding a woman of great strength and moral courage is not easy. She must be a pious and prudent woman, ingenious and industrious. She must seek only the best for her family and take care of her household. She must be a woman who walks side by side with her mate, helping and supporting him every step of the way. She must be a woman of spirit who can bear crosses with her mate and lift him up at every opportunity. For a man must truly trust and rely on his wife's love and skill if she is a virtuous woman.

There is truth in the phrase, *"Behind every good man is a good woman."* It is the wise woman who can get exactly what she wants in a manner pleasing to God.

Proverbs 12:4 says, *"A virtuous woman is a crown unto her husband."* Can you imagine being the kind of woman your husband cherishes, who respects and supports your every move, your dreams, your wants, and your desires? Can you imagine a man whose total reason for being aside from loving God is to please you? Do you ever wonder whether or not this kind of love is possible? Believe me, this kind of love exists when we live as this virtuous woman described in Proverbs.

A significant double standard currently persists in the mindset of numerous women, including those who identify as Christian. On one side, there's a longing for a *"Prince Charming"* figure who will sweep them off their feet, place them on a pedestal, and treat them with utmost reverence and care. Yet, simultaneously, women also strive for independence. We want to be like the woman of the popular R&B song *"Independent Woman,"* who says, *"I buy my own diamonds, and I buy my own rings. I only ring your cell when I'm feeling lonely. The shoes on my feet, I've bought them, the clothes I'm wearing I've bought them,"* etc. Or the old saying, *"I can take care of myself. I can pay my own house note; I don't need a man,"* but so often, deep inside, these very same women are craving their soulmate.

Like many women, I yearned for satisfaction, completeness, and wholeness in my life. I embarked on a quest to find my *"Mr. Right,"* hoping he would fill the void in my heart. I tirelessly searched for potential partners, asking friends, family, and even coworkers for leads. I inquired about eligible bachelors and even joined the singles' ministry at church, hoping to meet someone special.   However, my efforts seemed futile, and I began to realize that true fulfillment could not be found in another person. As the Bible says in Jeremiah 17:5, *"Cursed is the one who trusts in man, who draws strength from mere flesh and whose heart turns away from the Lord."* I understood that my search for external validation and completion was misplaced.

I turned to God, seeking His guidance and wisdom. I began to understand that true satisfaction and wholeness could only be found in a relationship with Jesus Christ. As Psalms 16:11 reminds us, *"You make known to me the path of life; you will fill me with joy in your presence, with eternal pleasures at your right hand."* I realized that only God could fill the void in my heart and provide the lasting love and fulfillment I craved. I surrendered my desires to God and sought His will for my life. I prayed for His guidance in finding a partner, but I also focused on developing a deeper relationship with Him. I immersed myself in His Word, spending time in prayer and seeking the guidance of the Holy Spirit.

Throughout this process, I experienced a transformation. I discovered that my identity and worth were not dependent on finding a partner, but on my relationship with Christ. I found joy and contentment in His presence, and my desire for a partner became secondary to my desire to serve and honor Him.

As I continued to grow in my faith, I began to see relationships in a new light. I understood that a godly relationship is built on a foundation of mutual love, respect, and shared values. I realized that finding a partner was not about filling that void in my life, but about sharing my life with someone who would walk alongside me on my spiritual journey.

Through the guidance of the Holy Spirit, I learned to trust God's timing and His plan for my life. I continued to seek His will in all areas, including relationships. I prayed for discernment and wisdom, and I sought the counsel of godly mentors. I also realized that the singles' ministry, while not solely focused on matchmaking, could provide opportunities for fellowship and spiritual growth with other believers. As a result, I became involved in serving others and building relationships within the church community.

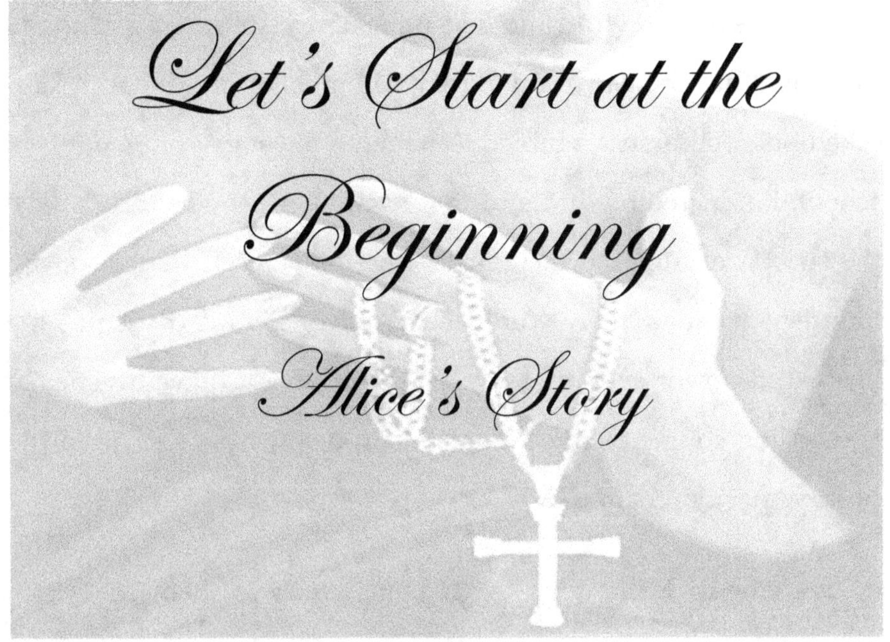

"For if our heart condemns us, God is greater than our heart, and knoweth all things."

—*I John 5:20 KJV*

I was raised in a household with strict rules and high expectations. My mother enforced curfews, limited phone privileges, and prohibited dating until the age of 18. Sometimes, she even monitored my phone conversations. Furthermore, we attended church services three or four times a week, a deeply ingrained routine in our family life.

Despite the structure and discipline of my upbringing, I longed to escape the confines of my parents' home. Feeling unhappy and rebellious, I became a troubled teenager, often engaging in fights at school. I'm incredibly grateful that back then, schools didn't have the strict "zero tolerance" policies they do now. If they had, my impulsive actions likely would have led to serious consequences like expulsion or even legal trouble. That would have drastically altered the course of my life, and I probably wouldn't be in the positive position I am today.

Looking back, I now realize that my home was not merely strict; it was rooted in godly principles, filled with love, and centered around reverence for God. It took me years to appreciate the values instilled in me during my upbringing. I lament the decline of such godly homes, where both parents and children alike embrace a fear of God and genuine love for others. These homes serve as beacons of light in a world plagued by moral decay and societal unrest. I hope and pray that we can return to the foundational principles of faith, love, and reverence for God, restoring the sanctity of the family unit.

At the time, I was experiencing depression without fully realizing it was a result of other problems in my life. As a child, I was sexually assaulted by a "friend" of the family while my dad was with my mother while she was undergoing surgery. Anyone who has been through this will realize the long-term consequences for survivors that affect their mental, emotional, and physical health. That experience is something I have never told anyone before, but I am now sharing it with you. I believe I put myself in a situation that enabled this to happen. I felt terrible and humiliated to discuss it. It wasn't until later in life that I realized the rape was not my fault.

The trauma of the rape left deep scars. I became hyper-vigilant, suspicious of every man I met. Their words felt hollow, their intentions suspect. I couldn't shake the feeling that I was unsafe. The shame and pain were overwhelming, and I internalized them, believing I couldn't share this burden with anyone. This secret festered for years, and the wound never fully healed.

The pain resurfaced with agonizing intensity when, as an adult, I experienced acquaintance rape. It was a brutal reminder that even those we know can betray our trust. The silence surrounding acquaintance rape made me feel even more isolated and unheard. These two devastating assaults led me to construct towering emotional walls, seemingly impenetrable barriers to protect myself from further harm. I kept everyone at arm's length, afraid to let anyone get too close. It seemed like these walls would never come down until I met the man I call "*my Boaz*." He was different. He was patient, kind, and understanding. He slowly chipped away at my defenses, earning my trust and showing me that not all men were the same. He helped me to heal and to believe in love again.

The First Mistake

Then shalt thou call, and the Lord shall answer, thou shall cry, and he shall say, here I [am].

—Isaiah 58:9 KJV

Due to my bitterness and perceived unhappiness, I hastily married the first man who showed interest in me, setting off a series of mistakes in my relationships. Ignoring wise counsel, including the proverb advising us to heed instruction for future wisdom, I wed at 18 against my mother's wishes, believing in my invincibility. I endured eight tumultuous years, during which my husband's alcoholism and jealousy escalated to abuse.

Despite attending church regularly, I felt increasingly distant from God, convinced my past mistakes had severed our connection. While I participated in church activities, I lacked a deep spiritual understanding. In the sixth year of marriage, my husband's baseless jealousy led to worsened abuse, pushing me into an affair with a man I did not truly care for. I rationalized it as a response to my husband's mistreatment.

Repeatedly leaving and returning to my husband as a result of my religious beliefs, I acknowledged the painful cycle of abuse. I advocate for specialized support for abused women within churches, recognizing the crucial role they play in ministering to individuals in such situations.

Despite my ongoing struggles with my abusive husband and feelings of turmoil, low self-esteem, and disobedience to God, I discovered I was pregnant. In the midst of my turmoil and disobedience, God blessed me with a wonderful son who became one of the joys of my life. Caring for him and experiencing deep love for him, I yearned for a better life for him and a positive father figure to mentor him.

My frustration with my circumstances grew as I longed for improvement and stability in my life. During this tumultuous period, I sought solace and guidance by confiding in my mother, the pastor, and the bishop of our church, as well as anyone who would lend an ear.

Desperate for answers and understanding, I turned to those whom I believed could offer help. However, I encountered resistance and rigid beliefs rooted in tradition and religious doctrine. Despite my pleas for assistance, I was told that I was obligated to remain in the abusive relationship, as leaving would be deemed unacceptable and could jeopardize my salvation.

"Husbands, love your wives, even as Christ also loved the church, and gave Himself for it."

—*Ephesians 5:25 KJV*

Understanding my upbringing is essential to grasping the reasoning behind those responses from those who opposed divorce. Raised in a Pentecostal Church, I was taught that divorce was only permissible in cases of adultery. Since my husband had not committed adultery, according to this belief system, I had no legitimate grounds for seeking separation or divorce. Instead, I was expected to endure the abuse silently, conforming to the role of a submissive wife, or face blame for supposedly provoking the mistreatment.

I vividly recall the moment when suffering a black eye and broken ribs, the bishop posed a disturbing question: *"What did you do to provoke this?"* Can you believe that? Can you imagine enduring such scrutiny and victim-blaming? In the depths of my despair, I prayed with an intensity I had never before known, yearning for genuine answers. I grappled with conflicting teachings that divorce was only permissible in cases of adultery and that God abhorred divorce.

Questions flooded my mind: Why would a loving God want His child to endure such suffering? Doesn't He desire our happiness? The scripture urging husbands to love their wives as Christ loves the church echoed in my thoughts, prompting me to question the nature of love in my abusive relationship. Was this truly the way God intended His children to be treated? I sought solace in God's kindness and the promise of a lighter burden, as stated in Matthew 11:30 which says, *"Seek comfort in God's benevolence and the promise of a lighter burden."* Also, in Matthew 11:30, *"For my yoke is easy, and my burden is light."* I looked to Him for guidance and insight.

In a profound moment, I felt God's voice resonate within me, reassuring me of His love and expressing His desire for my well-being. Though I believe God had been communicating with me all along, it was only then that I truly listened with a spiritual ear and heard His message clearly. He guided me to reflect on Malachi 2:13-16, where He addresses the mistreatment of spouses and disregards the offerings of those who inflict pain upon their partners. This passage illuminated God's deep concern for the sanctity of marriage and His disdain for its violation and abuse. I understood that the essence of marriage, as ordained by God, lies not in legal documents, but in the purity and sincerity of the relationship's heart.

God looks beyond the surface and examines the core of the matter. He made it evident to me that divorcing my abusive husband was not a betrayal of marriage itself, but a necessary step to reclaim the oneness and wholeness that He intended for His children since the time of Adam and Eve.

God acknowledges that divorce may happen even among His followers. A believer who has experienced divorce or remarriage should never doubt their worth or love in God's eyes. When one spouse mistreats the other, whether through physical or emotional abuse, the sacred covenant of mutual respect and wholeness is shattered. Choosing to leave an abusive partner is an act of honoring the divine within oneself, as our bodies are regarded as temples by God.

After the Divorce

The Lord is close to the brokenhearted and saves those who are crushed in spirit.

—Psalm 34:18 NIV

My divorce was finalized in May 24, 1989 and my ex became a stalker who would not let go. After my divorce, I made a solemn vow never to marry again, convinced that my life was improving despite the ongoing struggles. However, financial constraints weighed heavily on me, making it difficult to provide for my 3-year-old son.

Approximately six months post-divorce, I met a man who brought joy and generosity into my life. Despite lingering doubts and bitterness towards men, I found myself drawn to him. He showered me with kindness, gifts, and financial support, alleviating some of my immediate concerns. Despite his reluctance to attend church regularly, he was a good person, and I convinced myself that our relationship was acceptable. As he provided for me and my son, I grew further from God, leaning more and more on this man instead. During the eight years of our relationship, I became increasingly detached from my faith, indulging in the luxuries "*Jim*" provided and forgetting the promises I had made to God in times of distress.

I stayed out of church for eight years, not remembering that God had provided a place for me to live rent-free. Despite my spiritual neglect, God remained by my side, gently reminding me that Jim was not the partner He had prepared for me. Looking back, I realize Jim was merely a deception orchestrated by the enemy, blinding me to the true companion God had in store for me.

You are altogether beautiful, my love; there is no flaw in you. You have captivated my heart, my sister, my bride you have my heart with one glance your eyes, with one jewel of a necklace.

—*Song of Solomon 4:7 and 9.*

There are many successful single Christian women. Those women I admire and respect. Many women have raised hard-working children and established successful businesses and careers. These same women give back to their community and to their church. These are women I sincerely hold in high regard, for they have made being single decent and an honor.

But other single women are not as positive. The more I attended church and became involved, the more I noticed that I was surrounded by Christian women who were bitter and lonely. They complained about the same things that women grumbled about who were not in a church and who didn't know or even want to know God. I wondered at the time, *"What is the difference between church women and non-church women?"*

Some of the bitterness began to rub off on me, and I began sounding like them. I would hear myself saying, *"All men are just alike. All men are dogs. Men can never be true to just one woman, so why shouldn't women sleep around like men do? Why is it that only married men are attracted to me"?* I began to say, *"I am never going to get married again,"* or so I thought. I remember a lady at church who had been married for 15 years and was going through a divorce. It was frightening to hear her say, *"Nothing is guaranteed."* And I never thought this would happen to me, especially so late in life. This was a Godfearing woman, a Bible-toting, tongue-talking, faithful woman of God. What happened? The reality of divorce rates among Christian Americans is reminiscent of the age-old cliché that calls into question, *"The family that prays together, stays together."*

When I contemplated the idea of dating, I felt a strong reluctance. The dating scene seemed daunting, with the prevailing expectation that men, regardless of their faith, were primarily interested in sex. Even men my age or younger seemed to prioritize sexual intimacy, often expecting it even on the first date. It appeared that as people grew older, both men and women were more inclined to assess compatibility based on sexual compatibility rather than an emotional or godly connection.

The prospect of dating leading to marriage was particularly unsettling for me. I feared becoming another statistic: a Christian divorcée. Witnessing divorces among Christians and non-Christians alike made me apprehensive about the permanence of love and commitment. I vividly recall another woman from my church, who had been married awhile, going through a divorce. Her disillusionment and disbelief underscored the fragility of marital bonds, even among devout believers.

Lord, thou hast heard the desire of the humble: thou will prepare their heart, thou will cause thine ear to hear.

—Psalms 10:17 KJV

Like countless women today, I found myself swearing off marriage, scarred by past experiences of marital abuse, hurt, and deep-seated fears. I convinced myself that true love was a myth, an unattainable fantasy. In the midst of this turmoil, I strayed from God, consumed by disobedience and crippled by low self-esteem. I harbored a belief that no man could ever genuinely love me, fueling a cycle of sinful behavior and further distance from God.

Each new relationship only served to deepen my heartache, reinforcing the barrier I had erected around my heart. A voice within me constantly whispered, *"No man could ever love you. Marriage could never bring you happiness."*

Despite coming close to the altar on a couple of occasions, doubts relentlessly nagged at me. I feared abandonment and betrayal, convinced that any man would eventually cheat and leave me. My past sins and the pain I had inflicted on others haunted me, leading me to believe that I was destined for a life of bitterness, loneliness, and unhappiness. While I had received forgiveness for my transgressions, I still felt the weight of their consequences looming over me, a constant reminder that redemption did not erase the scars of the past.

When you continue to hear and read about these experiences, you may ask several questions: Should I be married? Can a marriage really last? Is it really for better or worse? Sickness and in health? Richer or poorer? Till death do us part? Is there any truth to these vows? It is distressing that the divorce rate among professing Christians is nearly as high as that of the unbelieving world.

According to Karen S. Peterson in USA Today (March 7, 2000), the Census Bureau figures show that in African American homes, of the people between the ages of 24 and 34, 54% are not married. The Census Bureau also showed that in 1998, 11% of Blacks aged 18 and over were divorced. In all, about 36% of Blacks have divorced. And people are not getting married as often as they once did. The Divorce Magazine reports that there were approximately 2,230,000 marriages in 2005, down from 2,279,000 the previous year, despite a total population increase of 2.9 million over the same period. This marriage rate in 2005 (per 1,000) was 7.5 million, down from 7.8 million the previous year.

A more recent study in March 2008 addressed 5,017 Christian marriages and was conducted between January 2007 and January 2008. The study reported that 26% of evangelical Christians, 33% of non-evangelical *"born again"* Christians, 32% of other "born again" Christians, 28% of Catholics, 29% of Baptists, and 24% of "other" Christians are divorced. (The Barna Group, Ventura, CA). And further research with 3792 adults showed that when evangelicals and non-evangelical born-again Christians are combined into an aggregate class of born-again adults, their divorce figure is statistically identical to that of non-born-again adults: 32% versus 33%, respectively.

And then we hear of many of the divorces among our mega leaders and people who we admire, like Paula White and Juanita Bynum, and we have to wonder, *"Where did we go wrong"?*

For women facing similar circumstances and grappling with related questions. I want to continue my story. I, too, struggled to find solace and comfort, feeling heartsick and lonely. After years of bouncing from one relationship to another, still searching for love in all the wrong places, I finally had a moment of clarity. I realized that the root of the problem was within me; I had been content with doing things my own way. It dawned on me that it was time to relinquish control and start living the life God intended for me.

This transforming realization occurred when I heard Pastor Johnson of Living Faith Christian Center deliver a sermon about God's faithfulness to Ruth and how He showered her with favor. It was a revelation that caught me off guard. I wondered, *"Is there a man like this out there for me? Can God truly love me so much, despite all my mistakes, that He would send such a man into my life? Does God genuinely care about my happiness, even though I've drifted so far from*

Him? Should I heed his words? Can I really believe that God loves me in this way, also?"

These thoughts troubled me as I wrestled with the tension between my desire for control and my faith in God's plan. However, reflecting on these questions, I found solace and joy in my relationship with God. I deliberately chose to delight in Him alone and surrender my desires to His will. I expressed my weariness of navigating life independently and surrendered to His guidance instead. I prayed that if marriage were part of His plan for me, I would accept it, but for the present, I was committed to deepening my connection.

During this period, I dedicated time to nurturing my trust in God, leaning on Him as my sole source of strength. As I deepened my relationship with Him, I found the beginnings of healing taking root within me. Learning to prioritize seeking God in all aspects of my life became my guiding principle. However, mastering the art of patience proved to be a challenging endeavor.

Waiting on God's timing tested my resolve and taught me valuable lessons in endurance. I want to encourage all of you who are going through a similar situation. Life involves continuous healing as long as you stay close to God and follow His instructions.

In the New Testament, there are numerous examples of strong and successful single women God blessed and esteemed. Inspired by their stories, I aspired to follow in their footsteps and embrace my own journey as a single woman with faith and determination.

Realizing that being single can be a gift from God, I embraced this time in my life as an opportunity to wholeheartedly serve Him and others. I shifted my focus away from seeking a partner and instead dedicated myself to delighting in serving the Lord and His people. This shift in perspective brought me a sense of fulfillment and purpose as I devoted myself to serving God's children and positively impacting the world.

If you find yourself single, it's important to examine the positive aspects of your situation. Recognize that God may have unique and meaningful ways for you to serve Him as a single person. By seeking His will and guidance, you can discover your path and fulfill your purpose in serving Him in special and impactful ways. Trusting in God's plan for your life and remaining open to His leading you will allow you to find fulfillment and purpose in your singleness.

Faithfulness is central to what God desires from us. He seeks faith in His children, as stated in Hebrews 11:6, that says, "...*without faith it is impossible to please Him; for he that cometh to God must believe that He is, and that He is a rewarder of them that diligently seek Him."* This verse emphasizes the importance of believing in God's existence and trusting in His promises, especially for those who earnestly seek Him.

Let's remember that God's character is unwaveringly truthful. As stated in Philippians 4:19, *"God is not a man that He should lie."* His promise extends beyond mere provision; He assures us that He will supply all our needs according to His boundless riches in glory and fulfill the desires of our hearts. Also, remember that God is always committed to providing for His children, and His love for us is boundless. It's important to find contentment and peace in our current circumstances, knowing that our ultimate happiness comes from God. While no one else is responsible for our happiness, we can trust that God deeply cares about our well-being and will always provide for us.

Even during difficult times, we can find strength and resilience knowing God is with us. These challenges serve to strengthen us, equipping us to stand firm and support God's work. As I surrendered my life to God and delved into His Word, I grew stronger and better able to support and uplift those around me. This reaffirmed my belief that God empowers us to overcome adversity and become instruments of His love and grace in the world.

The Lord is good, a strong hold in the day of trouble; and he knoweth them that trust in him.

—Nahum 1:7

---

uring this period of turmoil, I experienced a revival of faith as I clung to the belief that God would guide me through the challenging times I was facing. Despite the chaos, I found solace in God's unwavering support. He not only revealed a plan for me to extricate myself from my toxic relationship but also revealed the perfect timing for my departure. He instructed me to prepare for leaving, but I had to wait until the appointed time.

When that moment finally arrived, I had to remain in hiding for almost a year to ensure my safety. This clandestine period nearly cost me my job with the state, as my abuser relentlessly searched for me, forcing me to take extended leave without pay. Yet, even in the midst of uncertainty, God's provision was evident. Although I was on leave, all my financial needs were met, preventing me from losing my job. This served as a powerful testament to God's unwavering care and protection.

So do not fear, for I am with you; do not be dismayed, for I am your God. I will strengthen you and help you; I will uphold you with my righteous right hand.

—Isaiah 41:10

After being invited to a church by a friend, I realized something crucial was missing from my life. Joining this local church meant breaking off an 8-year relationship because my partner refused to accompany me. This decision was incredibly difficult, as it was the first truly solid relationship I had ever experienced, providing vital support for both myself and my son.

Despite my deep affection for this man, his unwillingness to support my faith-driven journey was a significant barrier and forced me to end this relationship.

Upon joining the church, I became actively involved in the ministry, playing the piano and even teaching Sunday school. However, despite my outward involvement, I had not fully healed from the bitterness and hurt stemming from my past relationships, particularly with my ex-husband. Like many, I attended church services, enthusiastically praising God, only to return home feeling empty, bitter, and unsure of how to address the lingering feelings of loneliness and resentment. Despite holding a prominent role as the minister of music in the church, I struggled internally, concealing my bitterness behind a facade of smiles, shouts, and amens.

After spending about four years at the church, I encountered yet another man I believed was my knight in shining armor. *"Jay"* seemed like the perfect match; he was a nursing student with his own car, place, and a decent job. And, of course, he was easy on the eyes. However, despite these apparent qualities, Jay proved to be self-centered, prioritizing his needs above all else and insisting on seeing me only on his terms. He even expected me to foot the bill for my own meals, justifying it by claiming we had equally good jobs.

Though he professed to be a Christian, his behavior caused me more distress than any other man I had encountered. My own folly led me so far from God that I failed to recognize the warning signs. Had I only heeded the words of caution found in Matthew 7:15, *"Beware of false prophets, which come to you in sheep's clothing, but inwardly they are ravening wolves."* Perhaps I could have seen through the facade. Despite my blindness to the truth, Jay and I even began planning a wedding. Yet, despite my mistakes and disobedience, the unwavering love of Christ remained constant. His arms were always open, patiently waiting for me to return to Him.

For the Lord your God is he that goeth with you, to fight for you against your enemies, to save you.

—*Deuteronomy 20:4*

During our wedding planning, I expressed my desire to be married at my current church, but to my surprise, he insisted on having the ceremony at his church. This revelation caught me off guard, as we had been together for two years, and he had never before mentioned his church or invited me to attend services with him. Up until then, he had been accompanying me to my church.

Concerned about our future religious practices, I asked him which church we would join after marriage and where we would raise our children. His response was unexpected; he proposed that our children could attend his church occasionally, but they would primarily be members of my church. He seemed unconcerned about the fact that we would be attending two different churches.

In the winter of 2001, as we continued planning our wedding, I experienced a profound revelation from the Lord. His voice, though calm, resonated loudly within me as if someone else were present in the room. He conveyed, *"This is not the one I have chosen for you. When you are ready, I will send the right person. Be patient and trust in Me."* This divine message prompted me to end the relationship, marking the beginning of my healing journey.

However, my newfound liberation was not without its challenges. Jay transformed into a stalker and made multiple attempts to harm me. I couldn't help but wonder why I consistently attracted similar types of men. Was it because I had failed to truly heed God's guidance? Or perhaps because I stubbornly persisted in following my own desires?

During my turmoil, Pastor Johnson delivered a timely message: *"When God lays out His plan for us, Satan inevitably challenges our faith and trust in God."* This revelation underscored the spiritual battle at play in my life. Despite the trials, I recognized God's hand, freeing me from this destructive relationship. Through this ordeal, I knew that God would reveal His intended partner for me, someone whom I could truly love and cherish.

Reflecting on my journey, I found solace in the realization that God had once again rescued me from disaster. It breathed new life into the lyrics of the song *"He Was There All the Time."* Even in moments when I couldn't perceive His presence, worship Him, or acknowledge His blessings, God remained steadfast by my side, patiently waiting for me to listen, obey, and return to Him.

Trust in the Lord with all your heart and lean not on your own understanding; in all your ways submit to him, and he will make your paths straight.

- Proverbs 3:5-6

After hearing God's voice, I felt a stirring within me, a deep hunger for His Word and a thirst for spiritual nourishment. Guided by His instructions, I made the decision to leave the church where I had served for four years. It was a significant step that I knew was necessary for my spiritual growth. I joined a new ministry where I encountered a pastor whose sincerity and honesty resonated with me deeply. Under his guidance, I began to uncover profound truths that had a transforming impact on my life. I was captivated by the teachings and yearned for more.

During this period, I wasn't focused on dating; I was consumed by a desire to know God more intimately. Serving as a musician in the church for three years, I found a safe space to release the pent-up hatred and anger I had harbored towards my ex-husband for so long. It was a pivotal moment in my healing journey.

As I delved deeper into God's Word, I consciously decided to stand firmly on His promises rather than seeking approval from others. Instead of pursuing human relationships, I devoted myself entirely to seeking God's will for my life. Following the example of Ruth's mother-in-law, Naomi, who provided guidance to Ruth, God impressed upon me the importance of preparing myself for the man He ordained for me. I surrendered my desires to Him, declaring my willingness to wait patiently for His timing.

In a heartfelt prayer, I confessed my exhaustion from relying on my own efforts and committed to trusting God's plan for my life. I rededicated myself to Him, embracing a newfound seriousness in my relationship with Him. I sought His presence with a fervor I had never known before, finding solace and joy in His Word and in His presence. Above all else, my focus shifted to pleasing God and aligning my life with His will.

For this cause, a man shall leave his father and mother and be joined unto his wife, and they shall be one flesh.

—Ephesians 5:31

My pastor often referenced Proverbs 18:22, highlighting the significance of finding a wife as a favor from the Lord. This principle is exemplified in the story of Ruth, who does not actively seek a husband but is found by Boaz. Proverbs 31:10 emphasizes the value of a virtuous woman whose worth surpasses that of precious rubies. Ruth exemplified this virtue, renowned throughout the land for her righteousness and honorable character.

Her decision to accompany Naomi back to Bethlehem underscored her loyalty and commitment not only to Naomi, but also to Naomi's God.

In Ruth 1:16, Ruth's unwavering devotion is evident as she pledges to remain by Naomi's side, embracing Naomi's people and God as her own. Boaz recognized Ruth's integrity and blessed her for her obedience and loving faithfulness. He acknowledged her worthiness, praising her for choosing loyalty over worldly pursuits. Ruth's actions exemplified the kind of character that garners respect and admiration, not only from Boaz but from the entire community.

Ruth's story serves as a timeless example for us today. Her commitment to righteousness and her selfless devotion to others resonate across generations. As we navigate our own lives, Ruth's example reminds us of the importance of living with integrity and compassion. Indeed, our daily actions and interactions offer glimpses of Christ to those around us, making Ruth's story not just a historical account but a living testament to the power of faith and virtue.

The story of Ruth exemplifies the profound themes of love and faith, revealing the redemptive nature of God's love throughout the narrative. Ruth's name itself means *"friend"* and underscores the deep bond of loyalty and devotion she demonstrates towards Naomi. Despite being released from any legal obligation upon her husband's death, Ruth chooses to remain steadfastly by Naomi's side, forsaking her own homeland and comforts.

Ruth's commitment to Naomi goes beyond mere duty; it is rooted in a profound love and respect nurtured by Naomi's kindness and guidance. Despite the challenges of living in a foreign land with uncertain prospects, Ruth's unwavering loyalty to Naomi reflects a deep-seated faithfulness that transcends personal convenience.

Naomi's love and care for Ruth likely played a pivotal role in shaping Ruth's character and devotion. Through Naomi's example, Ruth learns the importance of respect, love, and faithfulness in relationships. Ruth's decision to stay with Naomi, even in the face of hardship, illustrates the power of sacrificial love and underscores the foundational virtues essential for nurturing strong bonds in any relationship, especially marriage.

The story of Ruth teaches us that love, respect, and faithfulness are not just admirable qualities but indispensable cornerstones upon which enduring and meaningful relationships are built. These virtues - exemplified by Ruth and Naomi's bond - serve as a timeless reminder of the power of love and the unwavering faithfulness that it inspires.

One of the profound messages echoed in the story of Ruth is the deep concern and care that God holds for His people, encompassing every aspect of their lives: material, emotional, physical, and spiritual. As I reflect on my own journey and begin to pen this narrative, I keep God's care always in my mind and heart.

After giving some thought to the path that my life has taken, I have come to the realization that God has painstakingly shaped me into the person that He envisioned and that He continues to shape me even in the most difficult of times.

From my earliest memories, I grappled with feelings of worthlessness and a profound sense of being unworthy of love. There were times when I felt so overwhelmed by despair that I even attempted to take my own life. In hindsight, I realize that these struggles were more than coincidences; they were battles instigated by the forces of darkness. Satan, in his relentless pursuit to thwart God's plan for my life, sought to extinguish the flame of hope and love that God had ignited within me.

During this period of turmoil and despair, God's unwavering presence remained constant. He was there, gently guiding and protecting me, even when I couldn't see or feel His presence. It was His divine intervention that prevented the enemy's schemes from succeeding and preserved my life for the greater purpose He had ordained.

In many ways, my journey parallels the narrative of Ruth, in the sense that God's providential care extends far beyond the surface, reaching into the depths of our innermost struggles and triumphs. Just as He orchestrated the redemption and restoration of Ruth's life, God continues to work tirelessly in the lives of His children, ensuring that their purposes are fulfilled despite the adversary's attempts to derail them.

From Grocery Store to Soulmate

"For their redeemer is mighty; he shall plead their cause with thee".

—Proverbs 23:11 KJV

Boaz, a central figure in the Old Testament book of Ruth, embodies strength and humility. His name implies *"strength is in him"* or *"he comes in strength."* Throughout the narrative, Boaz is depicted as a wealthy man of quiet strength who diligently oversees his property, cares for his family, and demonstrates compassion for the less fortunate. Essentially, Boaz exemplifies integrity, compassion, and faithfulness, embodying the qualities of a true hero whose actions pave the way for fulfilling God's purpose in the lives of Ruth and her descendants.

During a time of famine, Boaz extends kindness to Ruth, allowing her to glean in his fields and instructing his servants not to interfere with her work. Recognizing Ruth's selflessness and devotion to Naomi, Boaz blesses her and ensures her safety and provision. As the story unfolds, Boaz emerges as the hero who orchestrates the redemption of Ruth's life. When Ruth is legally free to remarry, Boaz steps forward to fulfill his duty as a kinsman/redeemer. Through a process of negotiation with a closer relative, Boaz secures the right to marry Ruth, thereby safeguarding her future and ensuring her well-being. Ruth, unaware of the divine plan unfolding in her life, marries Boaz. Their union results in the birth of Obed, who later becomes an ancestor of King David, thus illustrating God's providential hand at work through the generations.

This seemingly coincidental encounter held deeper significance, a reminder that what may appear as chance occurrences often carry divine purpose. Like the Samaritan woman's encounter with Jesus at the well, seemingly coincidental meetings can be orchestrated by divine appointment. Reflecting on the story of Ruth, it becomes evident that her presence in Boaz's field was no accident, but part of God's meticulous plan unfolding in her life. Could Ruth's story possibly be a message to me?

God's plans for our lives are intricately woven, never left to mere chance. As the Psalmist wrote, *"The steps of a good man are ordered by the Lord,"* emphasizing God's sovereign guidance in our lives. When we surrender ourselves completely to Him, God orchestrates our paths, leading us to encounters and opportunities that align with His purpose.

Roy, i.e., my Boaz, entered my life at this stage. He and I had a brief conversation, and I took the initiative to invite him to church, exchanging phone numbers in the process. Throughout the week, he lingered in my thoughts, and when he didn't appear at church, I felt compelled to seek him out. Upon finding him, I extended another invitation, and this time, he accepted. Our communication blossomed, with Roy attending church with me and even helping out around my home. My mother, recognizing something special about him, grew fond of his company, often conversing with him.

Our phone conversations stretched into the early morning hours, with me mostly listening to Roy's words. Despite my lingering pain and reluctance to enter into another relationship,

Roy's engaging personality kept me enthralled. Over the course of two weeks, he expressed his conviction that I would be his wife, a notion I initially dismissed.

Unbeknownst to me, Roy had prayed for a godly woman and described his desired qualities to God, only to have me enter his life shortly thereafter. His prayers were specific, seeking a woman of strength, wisdom, and devotion to God, qualities he saw exemplified in me.

Reflecting on Ruth's question in the Bible, *"Why have I found favor in your eyes?"* (Ruth 2:10), I marveled at the unfolding of events in my life. It felt akin to a fairy tale, reminiscent of Cinderella's story, where a humble, hardworking individual finds unexpected love and acceptance. Like Cinderella, I had faced challenges and mistreatment but remained steadfast in my character. Yet, again, like Cinderella, I initially failed to recognize my Prince Charming when he stood before me.

And Adam said, This is now bone of my bones, and flesh of my flesh: she shall be called Woman, because she was taken out of Man.

—Genesis 2:23 KJV

Roy embraced the church community, renewing his commitment to Christ and deepening his spiritual journey. Engaging in Bible classes and seeking guidance, he appeared dedicated to his faith. Yet, unbeknownst to me, he grappled with inner struggles, battling dark demons that remained hidden from my view. Looking back, I realize that he carried these burdens when we first crossed paths but chose to shield them from me. In hindsight, I believe he saw our connection as a beacon, guiding him back to the path of righteousness.

Though he continues to face these demons, I trust in God's plan for us. With His unwavering support and guidance, we navigate this journey together, anchored in His love and light. While the road ahead may be challenging, I am confident that our shared faith will lead us to victory over these trials.

Life with Roy felt like a dream come true. We connected effortlessly, sharing similar tastes, beliefs, and a profound understanding of each other. It was as though we were destined to meet as if our souls had been intertwined for eternity. Roy quickly became not just my partner but my closest confidant, my best friend. We cherished every moment together, relishing in our deep conversations and basking in each other's presence. And even now, after all this time, we still find joy in our daily talks, as if we were still in the early stages of our relationship. When God orchestrates a union, there's a tranquility, a harmony that defies explanation. It's a peace that settles deep within, bringing an indescribable sense of joy, akin to a fairy tale unfolding before our eyes.

The revelation that Roy was my destined partner, my Boaz, was a turning point in my life. He embodies everything I ever hoped for, a source of endless joy, a pillar of strength, and a companion who completes me in every way. Roy is not just my life partner; he's my soulmate, my rock, the person with whom I can share every aspect of my being without fear of judgment.

Our bond is so profound that it feels as though we've known each other for multiple lifetimes. Others have remarked on how seamlessly we complement one another as if we were always meant to be together. Finally, I've allowed myself to love fully and unabashedly, secure in the knowledge that Roy cherishes and cares for me just as God intended. His love has brought down the walls I once erected around my heart, allowing my soul to emerge from its hiding place.

Roy's prayers for a partner were answered in me, just as mine were answered in him. He sought a woman of God, someone with strength, wisdom, and unwavering faith, a partner to face life's battles with courage and resilience. In me, he found his equal, his helpmate, as described in the scriptures, a partner to walk beside him through life's journey, bone of his bones and flesh of his flesh.

Trusting in Divine Providence

They are new every morning: great is thy faithfulness.

—Lamentations 3:23 KJV

Age has never been a barrier in our relationship. Roy has shown me that maturity transcends into numerical years. When Roy and I met, my son was a teenager, and their bond has grown stronger over time. Roy has stepped into a fatherly role for my son, providing guidance, love, and support. Their relationship is built on mutual respect and admiration. It warms my heart to see how deeply they care for each other. Challenges have been along the way, as is common in any family, but their love and communication have helped them overcome obstacles and grow closer.

Communication has been key in our relationship. In the past, I was stubborn and believed in my way or no way. But Roy has taught me the importance of effective communication. He listens attentively and asks questions to ensure he understands my perspective. We've learned to navigate challenges and understand each other better through open and honest communication.

I've learned that God is continuously active (sometimes subtly) to help us realize our Christian aspirations. My experiences that led to me ultimately meeting Roy is a direct testament to the Lord's protection and guidance.

Reflecting again on Ruth's story, I'm reminded of how God provides for us, even in difficult times. Just as Boaz instructed his men to leave extra grain for Ruth, God ensures our needs are abundantly met. Even through trials and tribulations, God's provision is evident, reaffirming our faith in His unwavering care and love.

God is capable of working wonders both in our present lives and in eternity if we turn to Him wholeheartedly, not just in our emotions but also in our actions. Like Ruth, I never harbored bitterness towards God, despite the trials and challenges I faced.

I've learned that although life may bring hardships, doubts, and uncertainties, remaining steadfast in faith will always lead to divine rewards. Putting God first in our lives leads to blessings and prepares us for our journey, whether or not we find a soulmate. Looking back, I realize that if I had been more attentive and obedient, my soulmate might have entered my life sooner.

The story of Ruth illustrates, as I've experienced firsthand, that genuine trust, obedience, and unwavering faith in God are met with divine blessings. As Matthew 6:4 reminds us, God sees our actions done in secret and rewards us openly. God desires our happiness and fulfillment, and when we prioritize Him and His teachings, He fulfills the desires of our hearts, as stated in Psalms 37:4.

As I immersed myself in seeking God's will, He prepared me for the companion He had in store for me. God transformed my life from one of emptiness and frustration to one filled with purpose, joy, and fulfillment. Throughout my journey, I've come to understand that the solution lies not in distancing myself from God but in drawing closer to Him in honest repentance. I've learned that nothing in the lives of God's children happens by chance; every event is divinely orchestrated and ordained by God. Though Roy didn't appear in my life until I released all the pain, hurt, anger, and bitterness from my past, God's timing proved perfect in orchestrating our meeting. This is the story of God's unfolding plan for my life.

Despite my rebelliousness and insistence on my own way, God was always present, patiently waiting for me to turn to Him. I share this narrative to encourage others to accept the truth that God has a purpose for each of our lives. If there's one takeaway from my story, let it be this: I firmly believe that when we surrender our lives completely to God, He reveals His plan for us. Nothing in life happens by mere chance; God's guiding hand is always there, leading and directing us if we're willing to listen. As Psalms 37:23 states, *"The steps of a righteous man are ordered by the Lord, and He delights in His ways."* When we acknowledge Him, He guides our paths, as Proverbs 3:6 affirms.

God has assigned a mission for my Boaz and me in His kingdom. Roy and I are the soul mates and lifelong partners God intended for each other. Today, we rejoice in our marriage, knowing that God has favored and blessed us. The Bible teaches that God shows no favoritism; what He does for one, He will do for others who place their trust and dependence on Him. So, whether your Boaz or Ruth is yet to be found, trust in God's timing and plan for your life.

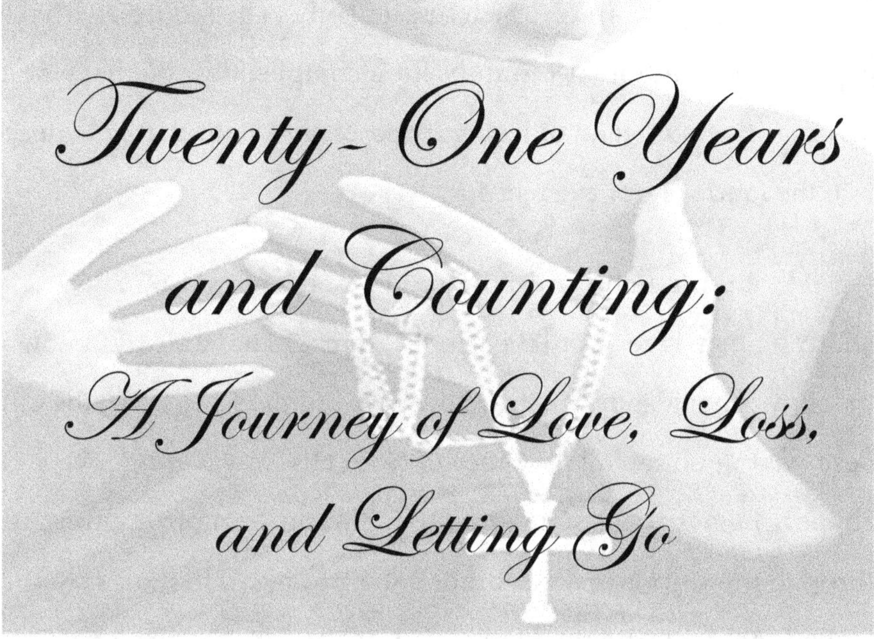

The steps of a good man are ordered by the LORD: and he delighteth in his way.

—Psalms 37:23

It is truly astonishing to realize that 21 years have passed since the beginning of the journey with Roy. Reflecting on this milestone, I am overwhelmed with many emotions and memories, unsure where to begin. We have navigated countless trials and tribulations throughout these years, facing both joys and sorrows. From enduring surgeries and grappling with medical and weight-related challenges to venturing into numerous business endeavors (some marked by success and others by failure), we have experienced the full spectrum of life's complexities. We have also endured the heartache of losing loved ones, a pain that cuts deep into the fabric of our existence.

Yet, amid the ebb and flow of life, one constant remains: our enduring marriage. From the very beginning, I have always known that Roy is not just my husband but my soulmate, my Boaz, the gift bestowed upon me by the grace of God. His unwavering love and support have been a source of strength and comfort, guiding us through the storms and celebrating the triumphs. In him, I see the embodiment of divine blessing, a testament to our Creator's boundless grace and goodness.

When you inquire about the experiences of numerous individuals, be they successful figures such as movie stars, singers, or actors, the prevailing sentiment often revolves around a resolute affirmation: they would not trade their journey for anything in the world.

However, reflecting upon my own life, there are indeed aspects I would change. I would prioritize the simple yet profound gestures of affection, ensuring that each embrace and kiss is savored and every moment spent in each other's presence is cherished. Instead of being consumed by an incessant work ethic, often tethered to grueling hours between 10-to-12 hours a day, I would dedicate more of that time to nurturing the bond with my partner.

Together, we would revel in shared passions and activities, luxuriating in the joy of companionship. Regret weighs heavily as I contemplate the missed opportunities for connection (i.e., moments to love, to laugh, to cry) particularly poignant as loved ones depart this world with increasing frequency. I now recognize the folly of taking life too seriously, understanding that despite life's trials and tribulations, a richness exists in embracing levity and spontaneity. While some assert that every experience is imbued with divine purpose, attributing it solely to God's design, I contend that such assertions capture only a fraction of life's intricate tapestry.

This section was originally written on February 16, 2019, as Roy, a member of the National Guard, prepared for a 1-year deployment. Even then, we wondered how this experience would shape us. He returned just last week, February 8, 2020, after a 3-week training period. The upcoming deployment is both exciting and deeply unsettling. We have never been apart this long. Most people who know us understand that we are inseparable: at work, home, everything. I know his absence will feel like I am missing a piece of myself.

Amidst the whirlwind of changes and challenges, another significant transition loomed on the horizon. My son, Cliford, is preparing to move to California. His decision to embark on this new chapter of his life fills me with a mixture of emotions: joy, pride, and a tinge of apprehension. While I wholeheartedly believe in Cliford and admire his courage to pursue his dreams, I wish the distance between us was not so vast.

As a parent, it is natural to harbor concerns for our children, and I find myself grappling with concern about Cliford's well-being as he ventures into the unknown. I fear that his trusting nature and willingness to accept others may make him vulnerable to exploitation or harm. Nevertheless, despite these apprehensions, I am reminded of the importance of entrusting him to God's care. I find solace in the power of prayer, knowing that God's protective hand will guide and shield Cliford as he follows his heart.

While the prospect of Cliford's departure fills me with a sense of longing and uncertainty, I am also filled with hope for the bright future that awaits him. His determination to pursue his dreams, coupled with his unwavering faith, fills me with confidence in his ability to navigate the challenges that lie ahead. Thus, as I prepare to bid farewell to my son, I hold onto the belief that distance may separate us physically, but it can never diminish the love and support that will forever bind us together.

With each passing day, I pray for Cliford's safety, happiness, and success, trusting in God's divine plan to guide his footsteps along the path of his dreams.

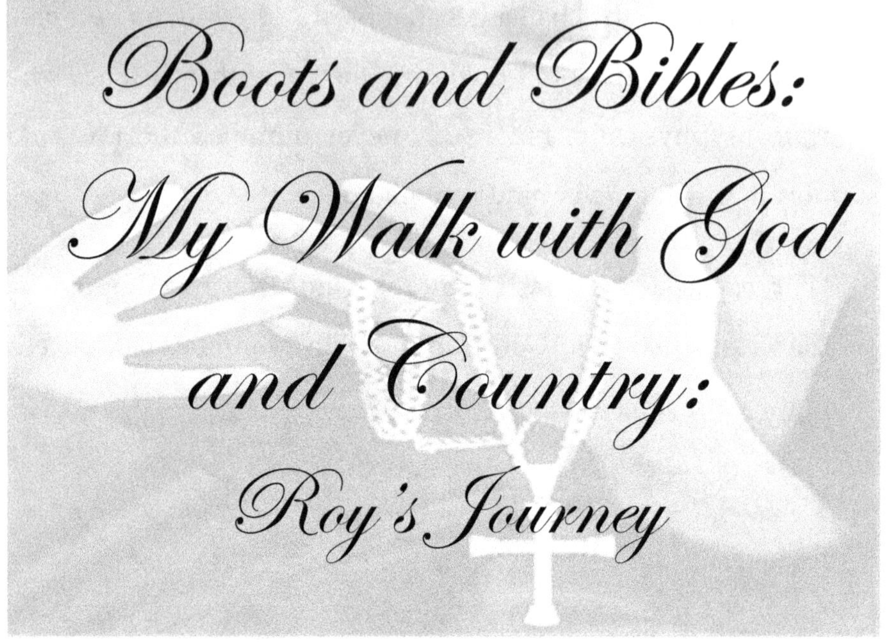

Children are a heritage from the Lord, offspring a reward from him.

—Psalms 127:3

Growing up, my mother's deep involvement in the Baptist Church instilled many of the beliefs I hold dear today. Although she encouraged my brother and me to attend, we did not participate in church attendance as often as she did. Nevertheless, she consistently ensured that my younger brother and I knew the importance of frequently attending Sunday School and vacation Bible school. Her unwavering faith and encouragement played a crucial role in shaping me into the man I am today. Thanks to my mother's influence, I became a youth usher at Fairview Baptist Church, where she remained a dedicated member until she moved to St. Louis to be with the rest of our family. I cherished my role, joyfully guiding members and visitors to their seats and assisting with the offering during youth Sundays.

My father's relationship with faith was complicated and inconsistent. Although he professed to be a Christian, his actions often betrayed his beliefs. He attended church only once a month for communion and struggled with alcoholism, which led to verbal, emotional, and, at times, physical abuse towards my mother. His faith seemed at odds with his behavior, reflecting a broader disconnect between his professed beliefs and daily actions.

He was a product of his era and upbringing: an African American man from the Southern states, 20 years older than my mother. Raised in a generation that valued stoic masculinity, he conformed to a tradition that discouraged open displays of affection. In his world, hugs were rare, and words of encouragement even more so. He wasn't the type to sit down to help with homework or engage in lengthy discussions about dreams and aspirations.

Despite his emotional reserve, I could always sense a profound, unspoken love beneath his stoic exterior. Even as a young boy, I felt his presence in quiet moments when he would watch me play from the sidelines or simply be in the same room. His love, though hidden and restrained, was a subtle thread woven through our interactions, obscured by societal expectations and personal struggles.

Tragically, my father never saw the man I became. He passed away during a tumultuous time in my life when I was battling addiction and making poor choices. The regret of not fully connecting with him, of never hearing the words of pride and love I longed for, has been a heavy burden. This lingering regret serves as a constant reminder of the emotional distance that marked our relationship.

Nevertheless, I carry his memory with me as a silent source of motivation. His life was characterized by emotional distance and inconsistent faith and drives me to break that cycle with my own children. I am committed to expressing my love openly and consistently, ensuring that they know without question the depth of my affection for them. In doing so, I hope to create a new legacy of warmth and connection.

Though my father is no longer here, I hold onto the hope that, wherever he may be, he sees the man I have become. I wish for him to feel a quiet pride in my journey, a journey dedicated to honoring his memory by being a father who communicates love and support without hesitation. Through this, I strive to bridge the gap left by his absence and fulfill a promise to myself and my family to embody the love and support that was once so hard to come by.

During those formative years, my mother introduced me to Mr. Jones, who encouraged me to join the Cub Scouts. The Scouts provided a much-needed escape from my challenging home environment, offering a positive outlet beyond simply hanging out at home.

I grew up in a lower to lower-middle-class neighborhood where violence was prevalent. Within a 2-block radius of my home, I tragically lost four friends to violence, drugs, and gang activity. Against the odds, I managed to escape the negative influences of my surroundings, pursuing higher education and dedicating my life to Christ.

Sadly, when I visit my mother, who still resides in the neighborhood, I witnessed its transformation into a drug-infested environment. Some of my childhood friends, now in their 50s, remain trapped in that destructive cycle due to alcoholism and drugs, with some having experienced jail time and even death.

Around the age of 11, I was fortunate to meet Mr. Lemar McNair, my Boy Scout leader, who became a steadfast and positive role model in my life. As a mechanical engineer working at a local chemical plant, he offered me a glimpse into middle-class life, inviting me to his home and exposing me to new experiences. Mr. McNair ensured that we had access to various enjoyable activities, such as horseback riding, deep-sea fishing, and camping. I vividly remember my first camping and hiking trip with him, where I acquired valuable survival skills, training, and a passion for community service through participating in food drives. Since the church sponsored our Boy Scout troop, we also engaged in ministry activities, visiting nursing homes with care packages and organizing additional food drives.

At around age 15, I was heading down the same path as many of my friends in our neighborhood. However, my life took a drastic turn when I was 13. I got involved in a neighborhood group that was involved in gang-related activity. Things escalated quickly, and I got into a verbal dispute with one of the boys in the group. I went home but later found out that the boy had gone home, gotten a gun, and ended up killing a 6-year-old girl while believing he was shooting at me. I was not even around when the incident occurred, but I was heartbroken by my involvement in the situation. That was a turning point in my life. I decided to change my environment, and, given my good academic performance, I transferred to a magnet school, which was a 40–45-minute bus ride away.

Attending the magnet school was a culture shock. It took me nearly 2.5 years to adjust, partly because many students came from middle- to upper-middle-class families. It was a completely different world with different styles, speech patterns, and life goals. Many of them had their futures mapped out with mentors and guidance. Eventually, I caught up, adjusted, and graduated 34 out of a class of 260.

Eager to leave home, I immediately went to college at the University of New Orleans, about 80 miles east of Baton Rouge. I completed one summer and fall semester there. With only $50 from my father and a small scholarship, I had to get a job at the dorm cafeteria during my second semester. The job was exhausting and made studying difficult, so I decided to join the Louisiana National Guard to help pay for college.

In the spring of 1988, I attended basic training at Fort Jackson, SC. After graduating, I returned home to Baton Rouge and moved in with my girlfriend. I enrolled in the engineering program at Southern University in the fall and worked as a waiter to support my studies. With the military's help, I maintained a good GPA and joined the Alpha Phi Alpha fraternity in 1990. The fraternity offered social activities and community service, which I found fulfilling at the same time. We participated in activities such as March of Dimes, helping people who were homeless, and collaborating with various organizations such as the Boy Scouts and the Big Buddy program. I formed some great relationships that I still maintain today.

I graduated with an electrical engineering degree on May 14, 1993, married my girlfriend of five years on May 15, and moved to Milwaukee, WI, on June 1 for a 6-month training program as a sales engineer with Allen Bradley.

Our marriage struggled with the rapid changes, but we sought counseling and persevered. After six months, I was transferred to Raleigh, NC. We bought a house, and life was good, but my wife became homesick. To help, we temporarily took in her cousin and her two children. My wife was lonely again when they left, so we briefly had her teenage brother live with us. However, he was troubled and caused problems. My marriage continued to suffer, so I transferred back to Louisiana.

With the business of life, we drifted away from church. Wanting some community connection, we joined a church, and I served on the finance committee, but our lifestyles remained unchanged. We were still drinking and partying. I was working full-time and had become a real estate investor, buying 13 properties in two years.

In 1999, our son, Roy Jr., was born. However, a year and a half later, we filed for divorce. I moved into one of my rental properties and fell into depression, isolating myself and engaging in destructive behavior. After about a year, I hit rock bottom and cried out to God. I prayed for God to help me recover and send me a helpmate who shared my faith.

A few days later I met Alice in a grocery store. She invited me to her church, Living Faith Christian Center. I missed the first invitation, but she persisted, and I eventually attended. There, I rededicated my life to Christ and began dating Alice. Sensing something special, I felt God reveal that she was my future wife and helpmate. She helped me with property settlements and other matters. I knew she was a godsend.

Alice not only professed Christianity but lived it. We grew closer and married. It was the beginning of my true spiritual journey. Alice introduced me to a new way of understanding the Bible. I had been raised Baptist but found this full gospel ministry different. I embraced her 15-year-old son as my stepson, and her parents, who lived with her, became like second parents to me. Alice quit her job, and we focused on real estate and our mortgage brokerage.

My true spiritual journey began the day I rededicated my life to Christ at Living Faith Christian Center in 2002. Soon after, I was baptized at my new church. To overcome my struggles with alcohol, which had worsened due to divorce, drama, and depression, I attended the Overcomers class offered every Wednesday night before Bible study. Alice attended with me, and we began studying the word several nights a week at home.

God is within her, she will not fall; God will help her at break of day.

—Psalms 46:5

After five years as a mortgage broker, I vividly recall the day I received the devastating news that the mortgage company I was working for was about to close. The office was filled with an air of anxiety as a few co-workers came to my office, visibly nervous and voicing their worries about what they were going to do next. One colleague, in particular, had just welcomed a new baby and had recently moved into a new home. Staff concerns were palpable, and the uncertainty of the future weighed heavily on everyone.

Feeling the pressure myself, I picked up the phone and called Alice to share the troubling news. The concern in my voice was unmistakable. However, in that moment of crisis, I was reminded of the immense value of having a suitable, strong, and godly helpmate by my side. Alice's words were a beacon of hope and faith. She said, *"Roy, I know you are not thinking about that. God is our source and our provider. Hasn't He always provided? He came through during some rough times when we did not know how to pay a bill or make ends meet. Hasn't He always been there for us? God is our source and our provider. We are going to be fine."*

Her unwavering faith and confidence were precisely what I needed to hear. Alice reminded me that our security did not come from a job or a company but from our faith in God's provision. She recalled instances from our past where we faced financial struggles and uncertainties, yet God had always seen us through. Her words were not just comforting; they were a powerful reminder of the strength of our faith and the reliability of God's promises.

Alice's reassurance helped me shift my focus from the immediate crisis to a broader perspective of trust and faith.

It was a pivotal moment that reinforced the importance of our spiritual foundation and the power of having a supportive, faith-filled partner. Her strength and faith carried us through that uncertain time, and true to her words, we found that God indeed provided for us, guiding us through the challenges and leading us to new opportunities.

Looking back, that moment was a testament to the power of faith and the importance of a supportive partnership grounded in God's promises. Alice's unwavering belief and her ability to remind me of God's constant provision were crucial in helping us navigate that difficult period. It taught me a valuable lesson about reliance on faith over fear and the irreplaceable value of having a godly helpmate by your side. I transitioned to life insurance. In 2007, nearing 40, I re-enlisted in the military, unsure why. Soon after, I began working with Alice as a real estate agent. But within six months, I felt a calling to attend seminary. I started at New Orleans Baptist Theological Seminary in 2008 and then continued my studies at Liberty University in 2009, pursuing a Master's in Divinity with a concentration in Military Chaplaincy.

Finding Our Place: A Journey of Service

Blessed are those who hunger and thirst for righteousness, for they shall be satisfied.

—*Matthew 5:6*

After some time, we moved our membership to Word of Life in Darrow, LA, where we became deeply involved in the church community. I served as an usher, and Alice joined the music ministry. We were actively engaged in various church activities and services for two years, fostering strong connections and spiritual growth. However, our lives were disrupted in 2005 when Hurricane Katrina struck, compelling us to relocate and find a new church home.

During this period of transition, we sought God's guidance and began attending Bethany World Prayer Center. For a year, we immersed ourselves in the vibrant community there, continuously learning and growing in our faith. Our time at Bethany World Prayer Center was a season of spiritual renewal and a deepening of our relationship with God, preparing us for the next steps in our journey, not realizing at the time that we were called to be evangelists helping with church growth.

Next, we were led to Voices of Faith, where we were ordained as Deacons. I worked in the media department, and together with Alice, we facilitated the couples' ministry, organizing meetings and events, and speaking at the marriage weekend conference. It was at this time that another minister that Alice knew contacted us for help in a new church plant in Zachary.

After prayer and discussion with our overseer, we were blessed to continue on this journey. Together, Alice and I developed a 6-week foundation class and organized the method and means of delivery, providing a calendar for the pastor to follow as he worked on the instructors. Shortly after that, I began my 3-month Chaplaincy Basic Officer Leadership course through the Army

Chaplaincy School. I graduated on August 19, 2011 and began my next semester at Liberty, where I graduated in May 2012.

During the classes, I learned more about daily devotion, sermon preparation, and working with people in crises. The critical thing I learned was working in a pluralistic environment and collaborating with ministers, preachers, and pastors of different faith groups.

I also learned much about dealing with people experiencing medical casualties in battle and how to minister to people going through their last stages of life. Also, during the class, we visited the University of South Carolina Medical School to view cadavers, preparing us for the realities of military service. We focused on the three principles of army chaplaincy: nurturing the living, caring for the wounded, and honoring the dead. This experience has greatly enriched my understanding and ability to serve in my calling.

I was endorsed in 2012 by the Coalition of Spirit-filled Churches, I was ordained at Holy Ghost Temple International Ministry by Pastor Goldman the same year, marking a significant milestone in my spiritual journey. This ordination empowered me to serve in various capacities and deepened my commitment to the ministry.

In 2015, I received a second ordination from Pastor Dr. Mark Litt of Greater New Galilee Baptist Church. At Greater New Galilee, I played a crucial role in developing the certificate program for the Precept upon Precept Bible School. This program was designed to enhance biblical literacy and provide a structured, in-depth study of the Scriptures, helping many members of the congregation to grow in their faith and understanding of God's word.

Father, do not provoke your children to anger, but bring them up in the discipline and instruction of the Lord.

—Ephesians 6:4

As a father, Roy has played an integral role in shaping Roy Jr.'s life. From his early years, Roy Sr. was actively involved in his son's upbringing despite being apart from Roy Jr.'s biological mother. He took on the responsibility of assisting his son's mother full-time, ensuring that Roy Jr. received the care and guidance he needed. Roy Sr.'s influence extended beyond familial duties; he served as a mentor and guide to Roy Jr., offering support and leadership every step of the way.

In his professional pursuits, Roy Jr. has followed in his father's footsteps, becoming a real estate investor like his father and acquiring his first property (a 3-unit apartment complex) at the age of 20. Along with his real estate ventures, Roy Jr. obtained his insurance license and worked as a licensed insurance agent to support himself through college, all while contributing to the family business.

Continuing his father's example, Roy Jr. joined the Louisiana Army National Guard, where he swiftly rose through the ranks at a remarkably young age to become a staff sergeant. His commitment to service reflects the values instilled in him by his father and speaks to his dedication to both his community and his country.

In addition, Roy Jr. actively supports the family's sober living house business, playing a significant role in maintaining the well-being of the clients. Through his involvement in various aspects of business and service, Roy Jr. exemplifies the lessons and values passed down from his father, embodying the essence of dedication, hard work, and compassion.

A father to the fatherless, a defender of widows, is God in his holy dwelling.

- Psalms 68:5 NIV

Roy's relationship with my son Cliford showed me a different kind of patience, one rooted in quiet understanding and trust. He explained to me that love sometimes requires stepping back and waiting. There were moments when Cliford needed space, and Roy's attempts to connect were met with rejection. Yet he never forced the issue, never took it personally. This made me realize that I had been treating Cliford's teenage frustration as a problem to be solved, rather than as a natural phase to be navigated. Over time, I learned to trust the bond that Roy was building with my son, even when the results weren't immediately visible.

Integrating Roy into our lives as a stepfather was undeniably challenging. Blending families is rarely simple, and step-parenting, with its unique set of complexities, was no exception. We faced difficulties balancing our different approaches to discipline, coordinating Cliford's time with his biological father, and addressing Roy's initial hesitations. There were moments when our lives seemed defined by these obstacles, yet despite this turbulence, I couldn't hide my sadness over my father's illness or my anxieties about Cliford and Roy. The process was raw, messy, and often overwhelming, but it also marked the beginning of a new journey for our family, a journey on which we learned to lean on one another.

Roy's steadiness became our anchor during this difficult period. He provided a sense of grounding as we navigated the stresses surrounding my father's health and the challenges of family life. Roy never dismissed my concerns but gently helped me focus on the present, reminding me that even in the midst of hardship, there were small victories to celebrate. His calm perseverance helped foster a connection between Cliford and my father that might not have been possible otherwise.

The relationship between Cliford and Roy, however, required a different approach. Their early years together were filled with teenage angst on Cliford's part, while Roy's good intentions sometimes missed the mark. As a parent, I often felt the urge to intervene, to smooth things over, to step in and make things right. But deep down, I knew that Cliford and Roy needed the space to build their own connection, to figure things out on their own terms. It was an exercise in letting go, in trusting that conflict, while uncomfortable, was not inherently destructive. How they navigated that conflict would ultimately define their bond. There were days when the weight of my concern felt overwhelming, but I clung to the hope that their relationship was a work in progress. And indeed, over time, there were moments of breakthrough, moments of joy, when their connection deepened in ways I hadn't expected. Those moments were a testament to Roy's patience, wisdom, and unwavering commitment to our family.

Our shared faith and commitment to family were instrumental in guiding us through these challenges. Through open communication, boundless patience, and an unshakable love, we came to understand that we could build a harmonious, blended family. It was not always easy, but it was made possible by divine guidance and the strength of our shared values. Today, I am deeply grateful for the bond that Roy and Cliford share—a confirmation of Roy's wisdom, patience, and steadfast devotion to our family.

There were afternoons when my father opened up to Roy about his past, stories he hadn't shared with me in years. Watching Roy's unwavering support of Cliford, patient and steady in his presence, allowed Cliford to soften, to see a different kind of male role model, one that had been missing in his life. This created space for them to develop their own rhythm, their own language of respect and affection.

Through all the challenges, I came to understand that a family's love is a renewable resource, even in the most trying of times. Leaning on each other wasn't a sign of weakness; it was a way of harnessing the unique strengths each of us brought to the table. In his quiet, steadfast way, Roy was the anchor that kept us all steady, teaching me that sometimes love requires patience, faith, and the willingness to let things unfold in their own time.

Honor your father and your mother, that your days may be long in the

land that the Lord your God is giving you.

—*Exodus 20:12*

In the biblical narrative discussed in Part One, Boaz and Ruth's love story shows remarkable devotion and faithfulness. Ruth, a Moabite woman, accompanies her mother-in-law Naomi to Bethlehem after the death of her husband. In Bethlehem, Ruth gleans in the fields of Boaz, a wealthy landowner and relative of Naomi. Boaz is immediately struck by Ruth's loyalty and kindness towards Naomi, and he extends his protection and generosity to her. Ruth, in turn, demonstrates her commitment to Naomi and her newfound faith by following Naomi's guidance and seeking Boaz's favor.

Boaz, deeply moved by Ruth's humility and virtue, ultimately marries her, fulfilling his role as the kinsman-redeemer. Their union is a testament to their love for one another and their unwavering trust in God's providence and faithfulness. Through Boaz and Ruth's story, the Bible exemplifies the beauty of love, loyalty, and God's redemptive grace.

This is how I feel about Roy. From the beginning, Roy embraced my parents as if they were his own. His genuine warmth and respect made him the son they never had. I will never forget the countless evenings when he would return home from work, greet me with a kiss, and then make a beeline for my parents, engaging them in long, heartfelt conversations that often stretched on for hours. Roy's ability to listen, share wisdom, and inject a bit of humor into those conversations endeared him to them completely.

My father's declining health was a gradual descent into the unknown, marked by constant grief that unfolded in stages. It began with smaller losses, his independence slowly slipping away, followed by the erosion of his memories. Eventually, the looming reality of losing my father entirely became inevitable, each step eroding my sense of control.

As a natural planner, I thrive on structure, but illness defies any semblance of order. Watching this once vibrant individual slowly decline forced me to confront the stark limits of my ability to fix or protect. This helplessness often left me torn between frustration and despair, compelling me to emotionally retreat in an effort to shield myself from a pain too profound to bear.

During this period, Roy's devotion to my father only deepened. As my father's health deteriorated, he required assistance with basic tasks such as bathing. Roy never hesitated to step in, providing the care and support my father needed. His practical skill, combined with a gentle respect for my father's dignity, moved me deeply.

Roy approached these responsibilities with a profound sense of duty and compassion, often reducing me to tears. His unwavering dedication not only highlighted my own sense of inadequacy but also offered a poignant reminder of the enduring power of love and respect in the face of inevitable loss.

A Pivotal Moment: Battling for Our Marriage, Faith, and Our Future

Be sober, be vigilant; because your adversary the devil, as a roaring lion, walketh about, seeking whom he may devour.

—1 Peter 5:8

Reflecting on our journey, we recognize its complexity, a tapestry woven with threads of triumph, adversity, joy, and sorrow. In every twist and turn, we have come to realize that God's plans for us surpass our imagination. Despite the challenges, we walk confidently, knowing His guiding hand is ever-present.

I recall a pivotal moment that brings back vivid memories. It was a night we battled for our future and marriage, aptly dubbed **"The Experience."**

I reached out to Bishop Johnson of Living Faith Christian Center, and his wife graciously answered the call, as he was away. Through prayer, she conveyed his instruction for me to bring Roy to his office the next morning, a directive we promptly followed. She unwittingly became an instrument of divine intervention. The night offers a profound and significant example in our journey, a pivotal moment where the resilience of our marriage and our faith in God were put to the test.

As we joined in prayer over the phone with Pastor Johnson's wife, little did we realize the spiritual battle that was unfolding, orchestrated by the forces of darkness to derail the magnificent future that God had ordained for us.

It was only in hindsight that we came to understand the true magnitude of that fateful night. The trials and tribulations we endured were not mere happenstance, but calculated attempts by Satan to sow discord and despair in our lives. Yet, unbeknownst to us at the time, God was already at work, orchestrating a future filled with purpose and promise, a future where Roy would serve as a beacon of hope and comfort to our brave service members, shouldering the weight of their burdens as a platoon chaplain. Little did we know that he would rise to lead a team of dedicated chaplains, guiding and supporting them as they ministered to those in the throes of unimaginable suffering and trauma.

In retrospect, that night served as a defining moment, a testament to the unwavering faith and resilience that bound us together. It was a reminder that even in our darkest hours, God's light shines brightest, illuminating the path to a future brimming with divine purpose and fulfillment.

As we look back on that turbulent night, we are reminded of God's faithfulness and the miraculous ways in which He turns our trials into triumphs, shaping our destinies according to His perfect plan.

Ye have sown much, and bring in little; ye eat, but ye have not enough;

ye drink, but ye are not filled with drink; ye clothe you, but there is none

warm; and he that earneth wages earneth wages to put it into a bag with

holes.

—*Haggai 1:6, KJV*

We hastily decided to join a church without genuinely seeking God's direction, a mistake that quickly revealed its consequences. Our finances were a constant source of frustration. Despite paying off debts and earning a steady income, money seemed to slip through our fingers. We were careful with spending, living modestly without extravagance, yet our bank account never reflected our efforts.

Then, Pastor Creflo Dollar's sermon, *"You are putting your money into a pocket full of holes,"* hit us like a ton of bricks. It dawned on us that we were out of step with God's plan. Though we faithfully gave to the church, our finances had not improved. We realized there might be a more profound disconnect between our actions and God's will for our lives.

This revelation served as a wake-up call, a stark reminder that obedience to God's will is paramount in every aspect of our lives, including our financial stewardship. With newfound clarity, we recognized the need to reassess our priorities and realign our actions with God's purpose for our lives. We understood that true financial health could not be achieved without being in harmony with His plan for us.

Thus, with unwavering faith and a renewed sense of purpose, we embarked on a journey to determine God's will for us. We sought His guidance through prayer, meditation, and studying scripture, trusting that His direction would lead us to where we truly belonged. This spiritual realignment not only transformed our approach to finances but also deepened our relationship with

God. We learned that true prosperity is not just about financial success, but also about being in sync with God's will, finding peace and contentment in following His path.

In time, as we aligned our lives more closely with God's purpose, we began to see some improvements in our financial situation. Our income seemed to stretch further, unexpected blessings came our way, and we experienced a sense of financial stability that had previously eluded us. This journey reinforced the importance of seeking God's direction in all areas of our lives, confirming that obedience and faith are the true keys to both spiritual and financial fulfillment.

Turning the Tide: A Story of Financial Redemption

A wise man thinks ahead

—Proverbs 13:16, KJV

Amidst a flurry of financial success, we found ourselves hurtling forward at breakneck speed, propelled by the allure of wealth and opportunity. However, in our haste, we neglected to seek God's guidance and soon found ourselves ensnared in a web of debt and uncertainty.

With money flowing in, we embarked on a reckless spending spree, acquiring land across the city with grandiose plans of becoming builders. It was a time of exhilaration and ambition but also of recklessness and naivety.

Then, in the midst of the chaos of our financial nightmare, a beacon of hope emerged in the form of a book: Dave Ramsey's "The Total Money Makeover." It was a revelation for my husband Roy, igniting within him a fervent determination to extricate ourselves from the suffocating grip of debt. His zeal for financial freedom was palpable, driving him to drastic measures as he sought to liquidate assets and streamline our expenses.

At times, it felt as though he was willing to part with anything and everything so long as it brought us closer to our goal. Part of our journey was faced with a severe financial crisis marked by debt, uncertainty, and a pervasive sense of despair. However, Roy's unwavering vision for financial freedom and relentless resolve drove our transformation.

Embarking on a rigorous path of budgeting and financial management, we meticulously tracked expenses, cut out frivolous spending, and made conscious financial choices. The initial sacrifices were undoubtedly challenging, but our intense commitment to our goals fueled our perseverance. Through disciplined effort, we gradually reduced our debt, with each payment bringing renewed hope and accomplishment.

As our debt burden lightened, we focused on building a *"financial firewall,"* establishing a strong foundation for our financial future. We explored various investment avenues, such as IRAs, mutual funds, the S&P 500, and other stocks, diversifying to grow and protect our wealth.

This journey was far from easy, but it forged a newfound strength and resilience within us. We learned to work together, communicate openly about finances, and face challenges as a united front. Our shared experiences deepened our bond and empowered us to face obstacles with greater confidence.

Ultimately, our relentless pursuit of financial freedom proved cathartic. We not only achieved our goals of debt reduction and financial security but also underwent a personal evolution. We emerged stronger, wiser, and more appreciative of the value of discipline, perseverance, and mutual support. What began as a tumultuous chapter in our lives ultimately unfolded into a story of redemption and triumph, a testament to the life-changing power of faith, determination, and the unwavering belief that all things work together for the good of those who love God.

A Marriage Tested: Overcoming Spiritual and Physical Challenges

For we wrestle not against flesh and blood, but against principalities, against powers, against the rulers of the darkness of this world, against spiritual wickedness in high places.

—Ephesians 6:12

Throughout our marriage, my body and spirit have faced a series of relentless battles. Various illnesses and conditions took a toll on my physical and mental well-being. However, as I look back, I realize they were not just physical struggles; they were a spiritual battleground.

One encounter vividly stands out. An older saint, now gone home to the Lord, shared a powerful message. She spoke of a great work God had planned for Roy and I and how it seemed to attract the enemy's attention. We were targets. Shortly after, the attacks began. We witnessed the first attempt through a near miss with an extramarital affair. When that failed, the focus shifted. Doubts began to worm into my mind, whispering that God was not real. It was a terrifying experience, a battle within myself against the very foundation of my faith.

Despite reaching out to trusted pastors and believers, I felt a disheartening lack of answers. However, years of Sunday school lessons, memories of the Sunshine Band, and countless youth church meetings became my anchors. Even in the deafening silence, I could faintly hear God's voice, a distant echo in the storm.

Through it all, Roy was my rock. He never wavered in his belief in me or God's presence. He researched alternative therapies alongside traditional medicine, tirelessly seeking solutions for my physical conditions. But more importantly, he held my hand through the darkness of doubt. He would pray with me, reminding me of the countless blessings in our lives, the undeniable work of

God's hand. His unwavering faith became a beacon, guiding me back to the light.

Those dark times tested us, but they also revealed the remarkable strength of our bond. We learned to fight for ourselves and together as a united front against the forces that sought to tear us apart. Emerging from this crucible, our faith was no longer naive trust but a battle-tested conviction. We were forever marked by the experience, forever grateful for Roy's unwavering support, and forever closer to God for bringing us through the fire.

While the saying *"at every new level, there is a new devil"* is not a direct scripture from the Bible, many of us have heard and experienced the truth behind this sentiment. Every time we overcame one challenge, it seemed like a new obstacle would emerge. We felt this particularly strongly in our personal lives, where my health became a battleground.

I faced a series of unexplained illnesses and ailments that doctors struggled to diagnose. The perplexing nature of my symptoms often left medical professionals scratching their heads, unable to provide definitive explanations. They would frequently comment that they had never seen such conditions in someone who did not drink or had not suffered a significant injury to the affected areas, whether it was my stomach, chest, or elsewhere. My answer was always the same: no, I had not experienced any of those things.

There was even a particularly memorable instance when I was scheduled for surgery. I had arrived at the hospital bright and early at 5:00 a.m., prepared for the procedure. However, just before the surgery began, the doctor decided to check one more time. To everyone's astonishment, he returned to inform me that they could not find anything that required surgery. He was puzzled, saying he did not know what had happened.

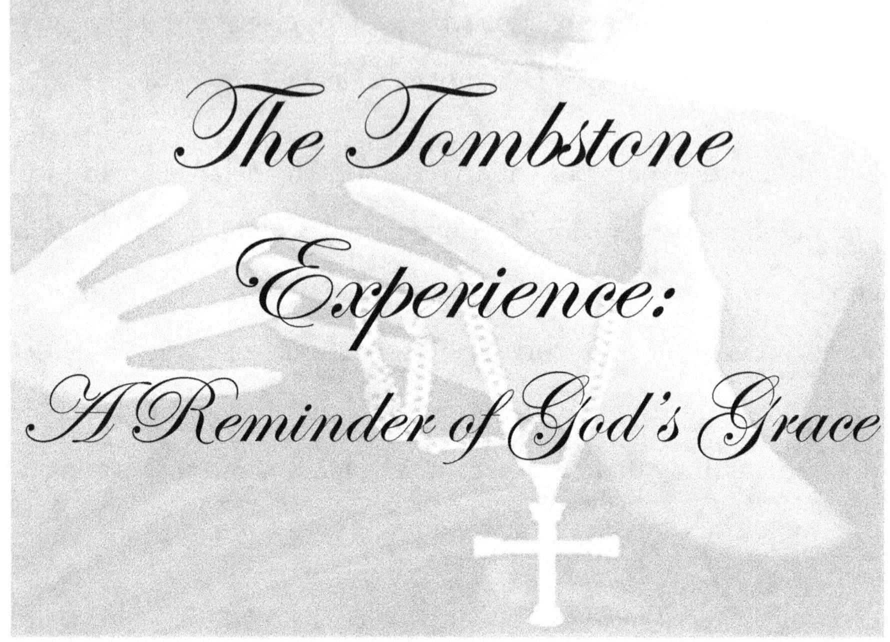

The plans of the diligent lead to profit as surely as haste leads to poverty.

- Proverbs 21:5

God gives us the gift of free will, allowing us to make choices that shape our lives. With this gift comes responsibility; our choices have good and bad consequences. While God does not want us to choose paths that bring harm or pain, we are not perfect and sometimes make mistakes. Even when we mess up, God's grace is there to guide us and help us learn from our actions. Romans 16:9 says, *"In their hearts, humans plan their course, but the Lord establishes their steps."* This verse illustrates how our decisions and God's plan work together in our lives. With that thought in mind, I would like to share what we fondly refer to as **"the Tombstone Experience."**

At that time, we were actively buying and selling properties. We were living on a spacious lot that already had two properties and space for one more. Without checking the city ordinances or property regulations beforehand, we bought a trailer to place next to the existing modular homes. We arranged for its purchase, delivery, and setup, only to find out later that we could not get an address or utilities for it because of city rules restricting additional structures on that lot.

The situation ended up costing us thousands of dollars between the purchase and the eventual removal of the trailer. Roy felt really down about the decision. But we have come to refer to it as **"the Tombstone Experience."** We have learned from this mistake, and now we can look back and laugh about it. It is a reminder that we all make errors, but what is important is learning from them and moving forward.

God's presence even in the farthest places.

—Psalm 139: 9

As I sit here typing these words, my heart is heavy yet again with the knowledge that Roy is preparing for his second deployment, scheduled for May 2024. The impending separation triggered a flood of memories from his first deployment when we endured the challenges of being apart for an extended period. Recollections of those days in 2019, marked by loneliness and longing, come rushing back to me. However, during the hardship of separation, we discovered a strength within ourselves and our relationship that we never knew existed.

During Roy's initial deployment, we navigated the trials of distance with resilience and determination. Despite the physical distance separating us, our bond grew stronger as we leaned on each other for support and comfort. Through letters, phone calls, and fleeting moments of connection, we found solace in the enduring love that tethered us together, transcending the miles that separated us.

As we prepare to embark on this journey again, I am filled with apprehension and hope. I take comfort in knowing that we have weathered this storm before and emerged stronger on the other side. Our experiences from the past have equipped us with the resilience and fortitude needed to navigate the challenges that lie ahead.

Roy's preparation for his second deployment and dedication to serving our country fills me with immense pride and love. The coming months hold uncertainty, but I find comfort in the unshakeable strength of our connection. The miles may separate us, but our love will forever bridge the gap. Upon reflection, it is surreal to see how God has orchestrated our lives. Roy, the young man I met at Piggly Wiggly, has blossomed into a respected Military Chaplain, now a Lieutenant Colonel. Never in my wildest dreams did I imagine this transformation, from a chance encounter to witnessing him becoming a Lieutenant Colonel.

The Unseen Hand: God's Guidance on Our Journey

And we know that all things work together for good to them that love God, to them who are the called according to his purpose.

—*Romans 8:28*

Our journey was and continues to be a winding road filled with triumphs and trials. Sweet victories were sometimes fleeting, followed by the sharp sting of disappointment. Yet, we never lost hope. Our faith in God and His more excellent plan fueled our perseverance.

The path was not a gentle stroll; it was filled with hurdles that demanded our strength and tested our resolve. However, within these very struggles, our faith deepened, and our understanding of God's purpose took shape.

Reflecting on our path, we see it was never meant to be a bed of roses; it was destined to be a rich tapestry of light and shadow, happiness and hardship. We discovered a powerful truth through every twist and turn. God's plan unfolds in ways far more meaningful than we could ever conceive. Though our journey may be difficult at times, we walk it with the assurance of His guiding presence.

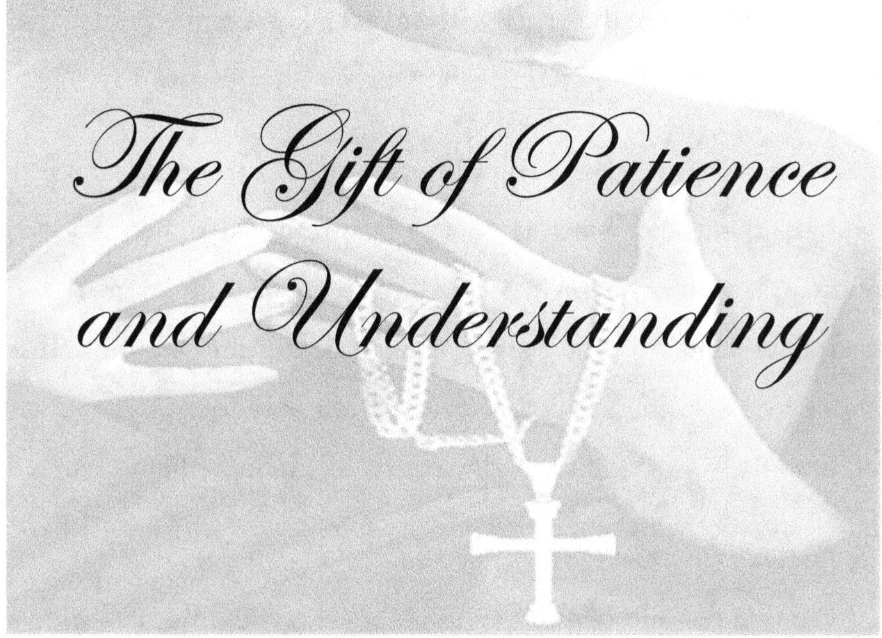

We then that are strong ought to beat the infirmities of the weak, and not to please ourselves.

—Romans 15:1

Roy has changed me in more ways than I could have ever anticipated. Perhaps the most profound shift has been witnessing his unwavering patience and understanding. With my parents, his ability to navigate their aging minds and bodies, always finding the gentle approach, made me realize how often my own love had been rushed. He taught me to slow down and savor the moments rather than rush to the next task. He reminded me that genuine care is not about efficiency; it is about presence.

With both my parents and Cliford, Roy has this uncanny ability to make them feel heard. He does not simply listen; he processes and validates in a deeply respectful way. He has shown me that it is not about having the perfect answer or a grand solution; it is about the willingness to bear witness, listen, and not fix. This ability of his to truly see people is a gift, and it has fundamentally changed how I interact with others.

Beyond his influence on my relationships, Roy has rekindled a sense of optimism in me. I have always been a doer and a problem-solver, sometimes to a fault. He has a way of finding the good, the potential, even in challenging situations. When I was overwhelmed by my father's health struggles or my concern for Cliford, it was Roy's belief in our strength that cut through the despair. He believes in the goodness of things, and that belief has become contagious.

Because of Roy, I am more patient, understanding, present, and hopeful. Seeing the way he loves my family has unlocked parts of myself I did not know existed. It has, without a doubt, made me a better mother, daughter, and partner.

There is a time for everything, and a season for every activity under the heavens.

—Ecclesiastes 3:1 NIV

---

*I*f you find yourself single, I urge you to nurture patience and trust in God's divine timing. Just as He orchestrated the beautiful love story that has graced my life, He holds a unique and extraordinary plan for your heart as well. Remember, God's love is impartial and boundless; what He has done for me, He is more than capable and willing to do for you. He longs to shower each of us with abundant blessings, and His timing is always impeccable.

Embrace this season of singleness as a precious gift. Resist the temptation to despair or lose hope if your "*Boaz*" hasn't yet crossed your path. Instead, use this time to cultivate a deeper connection with God.

Nurture your relationship with Him, delve into His Word, and commune with Him in prayer. Trust wholeheartedly that He is gently guiding you toward a future overflowing with blessings that surpass even your most ambitious dreams.

While you wait, invest in yourself. Grow in your faith, refine your character, and prepare your heart for the love that awaits you. Remember the story of Ruth; her Boaz arrived at the perfect moment, ordained by God. Similarly, your Boaz will appear when the timing is divinely aligned. Hold onto your faith with unwavering strength, keep your heart receptive to love, and fix your gaze on the One who holds your future in His hands.

God's plans for you are far more magnificent than anything you can fathom. Surrender to His process, cultivate patience, and have unwavering faith that He is diligently working behind the scenes to bring you the partner He has lovingly chosen for you.

In the grand journey that is our life, God has granted us the sacred gift of free will, empowering us to make choices that shape our destinies. Yet, with this freedom comes with a profound responsibility. Every decision we make has repercussions, both positive and negative. While God's desire is for us to choose paths that lead to joy and fulfillment, we are imperfect beings, prone to missteps and choices that bring pain and hardship.

But even in our moments of failure, God's grace abounds. He offers redemption and guidance, helping us learn and grow from our mistakes. As the scriptures remind us, "In their hearts, humans plan their course, but the Lord establishes their steps" (Proverbs 16:9). Our choices intertwine with God's divine plan, creating a beautiful symphony of human agency and divine providence.

So, let go of the worldly anxieties and impatience that often cloud our vision. Shift your perspective to a spiritual one, and allow God to orchestrate the unseen details of your life. He sees the complete picture, the intricate tapestry of your past, present, and future. He knows what is truly best for you. Trust that He is preparing both you and your future partner for a love story that will exceed even your most romantic fantasies.

In His perfect timing, your paths will converge, and you will experience the boundless joy of a love rooted in faith and guided by divine purpose.

-Your Love Story Awaits, Dr. Alice James

www.ingramcontent.com/pod-product-compliance
Lightning Source LLC
Chambersburg PA
CBHW060334310726
48976CB00007B/2556